Peppa Plays Basketball

Aberdeenshire

2145815

KT-573-101

It is a lovely sunny day. Peppa and her friends are in the playground.

Oooh!

JP
2145815

"Children," says Madame Gazelle. "Today we have a special person coming to teach you basketball."

Oooh!

Daddy Pig walks into the playground.
"Hello, everyone!"

"Daddy!" snorts Peppa. "It isn't home time yet! We've got a special teacher coming." "That's me!" says Daddy Pig.

"I'm the coach," explains Daddy Pig.
A basketball teacher is called a coach.
Daddy Pig spins the ball on his finger.
"That's clever, Daddy!"
"Peppa," says Daddy Pig. "Call me Coach."

Daddy Coach blows his whistle.
"In basketball, you bounce the ball with
your hands," he says. "Everyone try!"

The children practise
bouncing the ball up and down
the playground.

"Throw the ball through the hoop!"
shouts Daddy Coach.

Oops! George throws the ball the wrong way. He still needs a bit more training!

Daddy Coach decides
it is time to play
a game.
"Split into two
teams," he says.

The girls are in one team and the
boys are in the other.
"It's not fair," says Pedro Pony.
"We've got little ones on our team."
"Don't worry," says Danny Dog.
"The boys' team will still win."

The game starts.
Emily catches the ball with
her trunk. She is very good
at reaching up high with
her trunk.

"That's not fair!" says Peppa.
"Shh!" whispers Suzy Sheep. "She's on our side!"
"Oh yes, it is fair," decides Peppa.

"We want Emily in our team!"
shouts Pedro Pony.
"No arguing," says Daddy Coach.
"You can all be on the same team."

The children get into one big team.

"But who will we play?" asks Peppa.
"Erm," says Daddy Coach. "Well . . ."

The parents arrive to take the
children home.
"I know!" snorts Daddy Coach.
"You can play the grown-ups."
"But they're bigger than us!"
cries Danny Dog.

"Ah," nods Daddy Coach, "but you've been taught basketball by Daddy Coach!"

"Yes!" calls Peppa. "Let's play!"
"All right!" shout the grown-ups.

George tackles Mr Elephant, then passes
to Zoe Zebra. Zoe passes to
Richard Rabbit.

Yippee!

Richard passes the
ball to Peppa . . .
who throws it
through the hoop!

Boing!

The final whistle blows.
The basketball game is over.

Everybody cheers. The children's
team has won!

Hooray!